TAKING CARE OF MAMA RABBIT

With love to Leslie and Adam,
the best Mama and Papa
I have ever known

SIMON & SCHUSTER BOOKS FOR YOUNG READERS
An imprint of Simon & Schuster Children's Publishing Division
1230 Avenue of the Americas, New York, New York 10020
© 2014 by Anita Lobel
Book design by Laurent Linn © 2021 by Simon & Schuster, Inc.
For information about special discounts for bulk purchases,
please contact Simon & Schuster Special Sales at 1-866-506-1949 or business@simonandschuster.com.
The Simon & Schuster Speakers Bureau can bring authors to your live event.
For more information or to book an event, contact the Simon & Schuster Speakers Bureau
at 1-866-248-3049 or visit our website at www.simonspeakers.com.
The text for this book was set in Oneleigh Pro.
The illustrations for this book were rendered in gouache and watercolor.
Manufactured in China
1020 SCP
This Simon & Schuster Books for Young Readers hardcover edition January 2021
2 4 6 8 10 9 7 5 3 1
Names: Lobel, Anita, author illustrator.
Title: Taking care of Mama Rabbit / Anita Lobel.
Description: First ediiton. | New York : Simon & Schuster Books for Young Readers, 2021. | "A Paula Wiseman Book." |
Audience: Ages 4-8. | Audience: Grades 2-3. | Summary: When Mama Rabbit is not feeling well, her little rabbits each
find their own way to make her feel better.
Identifiers: LCCN 2020029439 (print) | LCCN 2020029440 (ebook) | ISBN 9781534470644 (hardback) | ISBN
9781534470637 (ebook)
Subjects: CYAC: Mother and child—Fiction. | Sick—Fiction. | Rabbits—Fiction.
Classification: LCC PZ7.L7794 Tak 2021 (print) | LCC PZ7.L7794 (ebook) | DDC [E]—dc23
LC record available at https://lccn.loc.gov/2020029439
LC ebook record available at https://lccn.loc.gov/2020029440

TAKING CARE OF MAMA RABBIT

ANITA LOBEL

A PAULA WISEMAN BOOK
SIMON & SCHUSTER BOOKS FOR YOUNG READERS
NEW YORK LONDON TORONTO SYDNEY NEW DELHI

One morning, Mama Rabbit stayed in bed.
That made her ten little rabbits worried.

"Where is Papa?" they asked.

"Papa went to get me medicine," Mama mumbled.

Medicine!

Mama did look very pale.

And not at all happy.

"We have to cheer up Mama,"
the ten little rabbits agreed.

One by one, they brought her:

A fresh handkerchief.

A steaming cup of hot chocolate.

A cuddly toy.

A juicy apple.

A delicious cookie.

A sweet-smelling flower.

A pretty ribbon.

A shiny necklace.

A colorful picture.

A good book.

Mama Rabbit looked much happier.
And not so pale anymore.

"Now we have a special surprise for you, Mama!"
the ten little rabbits said.

Just then, Papa Rabbit walked through the door.
"I have brought your medicine, dear," he said.

Mama hopped out of bed.
"Thank you, Papa," she said.
"But I don't really think I need medicine.
Our darling rabbits have made me all better without it."

The ten little rabbits lined up and put on a show for their mama and papa.

Mama and Papa Rabbit clapped and cried, "Bravo, bravo! We have the nicest, sweetest, cleverest little rabbits in the whole world."